Mudball

For Ava

First paperback edition 2011

The Library of Congress has cataloged the hardcover edition as follows:

Tavares, Matt.
Mudball / Matt Tavares. —1st ed.
p. cm.
Summary: During a rainy Minneapolis Millers baseball game in 1903, Little Andy Oyler has
the chance to become a hero by hitting the shortest and muddiest home run in history.
ISBN 978-0-7636-2387-6 (hardcover)
[1. Baseball—Fiction. 2. Minneapolis Millers (Baseball team)—Fiction.
3. Minneapolis (Minn.)—Fiction.] I. Title.
PZ7.T211427Mu 2005
[Fic]—dc22   2004040671

ISBN 978-0-7636-4136-8 (paperback)

19 20 21 22 APS 10 9 8 7 6 5 4 3

Printed in Humen, Dongguan, China

This book was typeset in Slimbach.
The illustrations were done in pencil and watercolor.

Candlewick Press
99 Dover Street
Somerville, Massachusetts 02144

visit us at www.candlewick.com

Mudball

Matt Tavares

CANDLEWICK PRESS

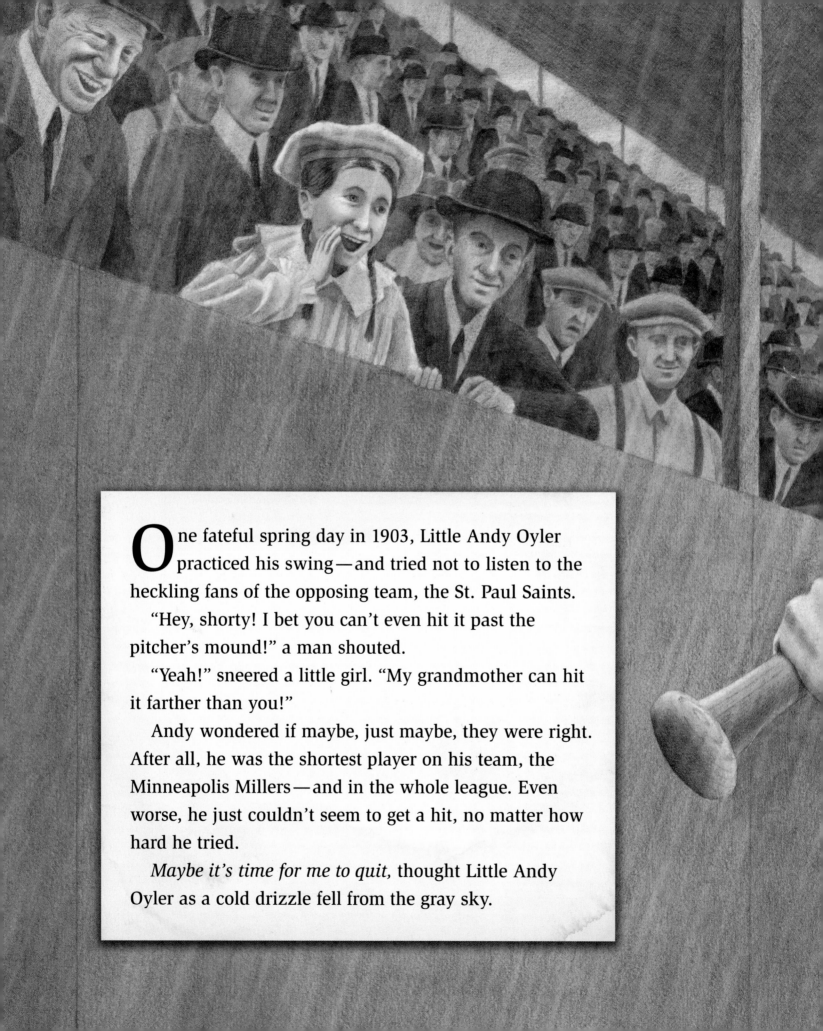

One fateful spring day in 1903, Little Andy Oyler practiced his swing—and tried not to listen to the heckling fans of the opposing team, the St. Paul Saints.

"Hey, shorty! I bet you can't even hit it past the pitcher's mound!" a man shouted.

"Yeah!" sneered a little girl. "My grandmother can hit it farther than you!"

Andy wondered if maybe, just maybe, they were right. After all, he was the shortest player on his team, the Minneapolis Millers—and in the whole league. Even worse, he just couldn't seem to get a hit, no matter how hard he tried.

Maybe it's time for me to quit, thought Little Andy Oyler as a cold drizzle fell from the gray sky.

The Minneapolis Millers trailed the St. Paul Saints by three runs. They were down to their final out, the bases were loaded, and Little Andy Oyler was their only hope. But just as he stepped into the batter's box, it began to pour.

"Time out!" yelled the umpire. "Wait until this storm cloud passes!"
But the rain kept coming, and within minutes the infield had turned to mud and the field was spotted with puddles.

"Play on!" the umpire finally yelled. He was hoping for one quick out, and with Little Andy Oyler up, he knew the chances of that were good.

Andy's cold hands trembled as he tightened his grip on the bat.

"Bring us home, kid!" shouted Maloney, taking his lead off first.

"Just keep your eye on the ball!" yelled Yeager, standing ankle-deep in a puddle, just left of second base.

"And whatever you do, don't strike out!" growled Slugger McCreery, wringing out his jersey at third.

The pitcher wound up and fired a fastball. But the wet ball slipped as it left his hand, and went hurtling straight toward Little Andy Oyler's head.

"Look out!" yelled Maloney.

"Duck!" screamed Yeager, covering his eyes.

"And don't strike out!" shouted McCreery.

Andy braced himself. But just when he expected the ball to hit him, he heard the unmistakable sound of ball against bat.

CRACK!

Somehow, Andy's bat had hit the ball. Everybody heard it . . .

but nobody saw where it went.

Little Andy Oyler took off for first.

"He popped it up!" the catcher shouted. "I saw the ball go straight up!"
He ran in circles around home plate, ready to catch the ball when it fell from the sky.

But it never did.

"I think it's in this puddle!" the first baseman shouted. "I saw it land right here!"
He splashed and splashed, but still the ball was nowhere to be found.

Meanwhile, Slugger McCreery strutted across home plate.
The score was 3 to 1.

"Oyler stole the ball! Check his pockets!" the Saints fans yelled.
Andy raced toward second, but the second baseman stood in his way.
"Come here, you little thief!" he growled.

The second baseman dove, but Andy jumped right over him. He rounded second and headed for third as Yeager slid safely home.

The score was 3 to 2.

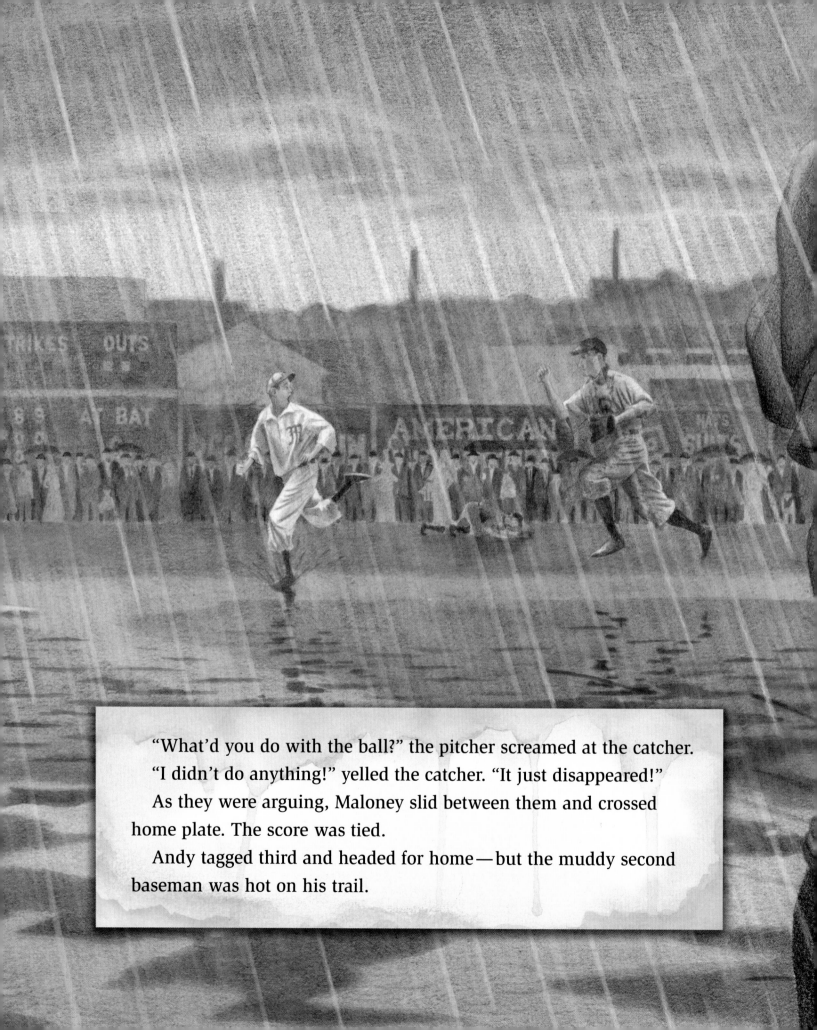

"What'd you do with the ball?" the pitcher screamed at the catcher.

"I didn't do anything!" yelled the catcher. "It just disappeared!"

As they were arguing, Maloney slid between them and crossed home plate. The score was tied.

Andy tagged third and headed for home—but the muddy second baseman was hot on his trail.

"I'm gonna get you!" the second baseman yelled. With every step, he drew closer and closer.

But just as he was ready to pounce on Andy—

he tripped and fell face-down in the mud.
Little Andy Oyler crossed home plate with the winning run.

"We scored four runs! We win!" yelled the Millers' manager.

"It doesn't count!" shouted the Saints' manager. "Nobody knows where the ball went!"

"Aaugh!" moaned the second baseman. "I tripped on a rock and twisted my ankle."

The umpire scratched his head. "There weren't any rocks when I raked the field this morning," he said.

"Oh yeah?" said the second baseman. "Then what's this?"

"FAIR BALL!" shouted the umpire. "The Millers win!"

The Millers jumped for joy. The fans rushed the field. And everyone crowded around Little Andy Oyler—the big hero of Minneapolis.

Epilogue

EVEN THOUGH HIS HOME RUN TRAVELED ONLY A FEW FEET in front of home plate, it seemed to break Andy Oyler out of his slump. He had three hits the next day, and by the end of that season, he was one of the Minneapolis Millers' best players.

The St. Paul Saints fans kept making fun of Andy for being short, but it didn't bother him one bit. He knew that he didn't have to hit the ball over the fence to help his team—he just had to play hard and have fun. And that's what Andy Oyler did, even on days when he couldn't seem to get a hit, no matter how hard he tried. Andy loved playing for the Millers, and the fans at Nicollet Park loved watching him play.

Andy Oyler never did hit another home run. But while other records have come and gone, no player has come close to doing what he did on that muddy day back in 1903, when the shortest player in the league became a hero by hitting the shortest home run in baseball history.

AUTHOR'S NOTE

Babe Ruth, the legendary New York Yankees slugger, was at bat during the third game of the 1932 World Series, when he stepped out of the batter's box and pointed to the center field bleachers. On the very next pitch, he smacked a home run over the center field fence. The ball landed exactly where he had pointed.

This tale of Babe Ruth's "called shot" has become an integral part of baseball folklore, even though many baseball historians question whether it actually happened. Several eyewitnesses insist that Ruth was merely holding up two fingers to signal to the pitcher that there were only two strikes.

Not everyone believes Babe Ruth "called his shot," and many baseball historians believe that Andy Oyler's muddy home run never happened. There is no reference to it in any early twentieth-century newspapers or magazines. In fact, the earliest mention of it came in a 1966 *Minneapolis Tribune* article. By that time, the tale of Andy Oyler's home run had been passed down through generations, and many baseball fans in Minneapolis had heard about the shortest home run in baseball history.

Over the years, the legend of Andy Oyler has grown. With each retelling, details have been added and altered. And what has emerged is a classic American folktale—the story of Little Andy Oyler, the underdog who faced his darkest hour and splashed his way to victory.

Even though these stories might not be true, they endure because they give us heroes we can emulate and Everymen with whom we can identify. Many of us wish we had the strength, skill, and unabashed confidence of Babe Ruth, and we can all empathize with the plight of Little Andy Oyler. Surely, we have all found ourselves in situations where we feel helpless, small, and ready to quit—but as Andy's story demonstrates, good fortune may rain down on us when we least expect it.

Bibliography

Bernstein, Ross. *Batter-Up! Celebrating a Century of Minnesota Baseball.* Minneapolis: Nodin Press, 2003.

Bryson, Michael G. *The Twenty-Four-Inch Home Run and Other Outlandish, Incredible but True Events in Baseball History.* Chicago: Contemporary Publishing, 1990.

Mona, Dave. "Nicollet Park: A Colorful Page in Baseball History." *Minneapolis Tribune,* November 6, 1966.

Thornley, Stew. *On to Nicollet: The Glory and Fame of the Minneapolis Millers.* Minneapolis: Nodin Press, 1988.